Entire contents © DUPUIS 2009, 2014 by Vehlmann, Kerascoët. www.dupuis.com. All rights reserved. No part of this book (except small portions for review purposes) may be reproduced in any form without written permission from Vehlmann, Kerascoët, or Drawn & Quarterly. Originally published in French as *Jolies Ténèbres* by Dupuis. Translator: Helge Dascher. Translation editor: John Kadlecek. Title design: Ray Fenwick. First hardcover edition: February 2014. Second hardcover printing: April 2014. 10 9 8 7 6 5 4 3 2. Printed in Singapore. Library and Archives Canada Cataloguing in Publication. Vehlmann, Fabien, 1972–, [*Jolies Ténèbres*. English] *Beautiful Darkness* / Fabien Vehlmann & Kerascoët; based on an original idea by Marie Pommepuy; story by Marie Pommepuy & Fabien Vehlmann; art by Kerascoët; translated by Helge Dascher. Translation of: *Jolies Ténèbres*. ISBN 978-1-77046-129-1 (bound) 1. Graphic novels. I. Kerascoët, artist II. Pommepuy, Marie, 1978–, author III. Dascher, Helge, 1965–, translator IV. Title. V. Title: *Jolies Ténèbres*. English. PN6747.V45J6413 2013 741.5'944 C2013-902356-9. This work, published as part of grant programs for publication (Acquisition of Rights and Translation), received support from the French Ministry of Foreign and European Affairs and from the Institut français. Cet ouvrage, publié dans le cadre du Programme d'Aide à la Publication (Cession de droits et Traduction), a bénéficié du soutien du Ministère des Affaires étrangères et européennes et de l'Institu français. Drawn & Quarterly acknowledges the financial contribution of the Government of Canada through the Canada Book Fund for our publishing activities and for support of this edition. Published in the USA by Drawn & Quarterly, a client publisher of Farrar, Straus and Giroux. Orders: 888.330.8477. Published in Canada by Drawn & Quarterly, a client publisher of Raincoast Books. Orders: 800.663.5714. Published in the United Kingdom by Drawn & Quarterly, a client publisher of Publishers Group UK. Orders: info@pguk.co.uk. *www.drawnandquarterly.com*

Liberté • Égalité • Fraternité
RÉPUBLIQUE FRANÇAISE

Beautiful Darkness

Fabien Vehlmann & Kerascoët

Based on an original idea by Marie Pommepuy
Story by Marie Pommepuy & Fabien Vehlmann
Art by Kerascoët
Translated by Helge Dascher

DRAWN & QUARTERLY

YOOO-HOOO!

IS ANYBODY HERE?

YOO-HOO!

?!

CRUNCH
CRUNCH

...THAT LOOKS REALLY GOOD.

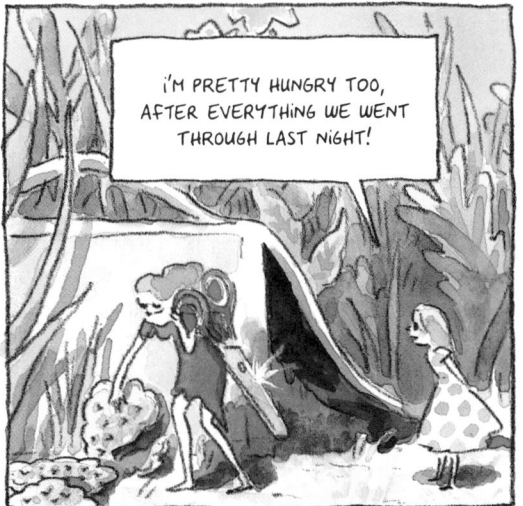

I'M PRETTY HUNGRY TOO, AFTER EVERYTHING WE WENT THROUGH LAST NIGHT!

YOU KNOW, I WAS JUST ABOUT TO SERVE CAKE WHEN THE CEILING STARTED TO...?!

GO AHEAD, HELP YOURSELF.

HEY HO!

?!

WHOA! WHOA! WHOA! COOKIES! AWESOME!

THANKS, PLIM. I'M HAPPY TO SEE YOU, TOO.

HAVE YOU SEEN HECTOR?
I HOPE HE'S OKAY.

NOPE, HAVEN'T SEEN HIM.

CAN I HAVE A
COOKIE NOW?

WAIT, FIRST GO TELL THE
OTHERS...LET THEM
KNOW WE'VE FOUND FOOD.

OKAY,
FIIIIINE.

RUN, PLIM! FLY
LIKE THE WIND!

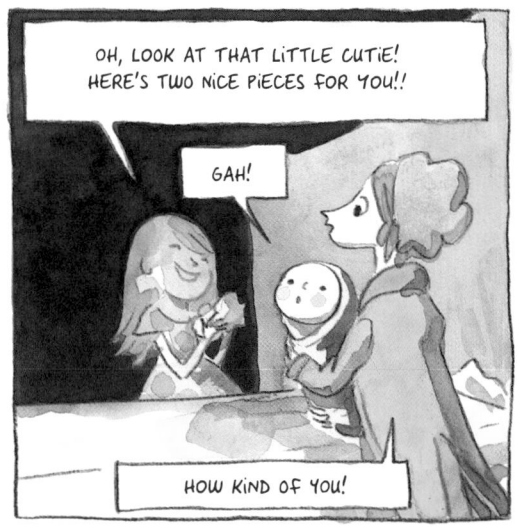

OH, LOOK AT THAT LITTLE CUTIE! HERE'S TWO NICE PIECES FOR YOU!!

GAH!

HOW KIND OF YOU!

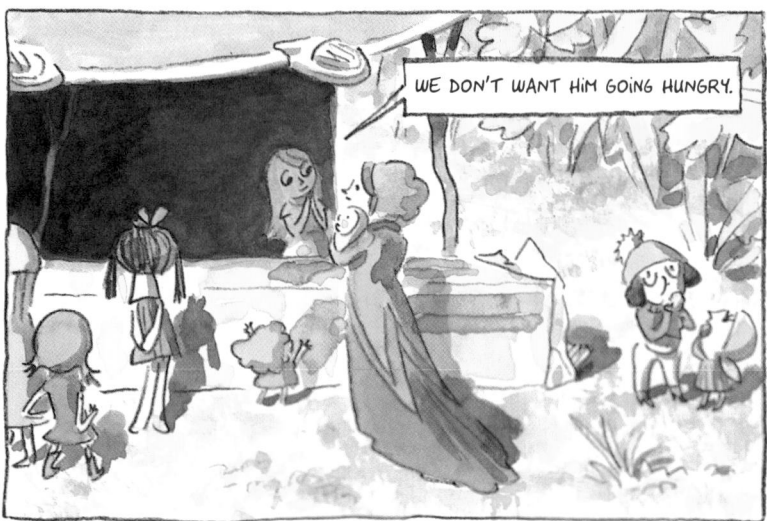

WE DON'T WANT HIM GOING HUNGRY.

HECTOR?

PLIM, CAN I LEAVE YOU TO HANDLE THE REST?

WITH PLEASURE!

BE SURE TO MAKE THE PORTIONS EVEN SO IT'S NICE AND FAIR.

UNDERSTOOD!

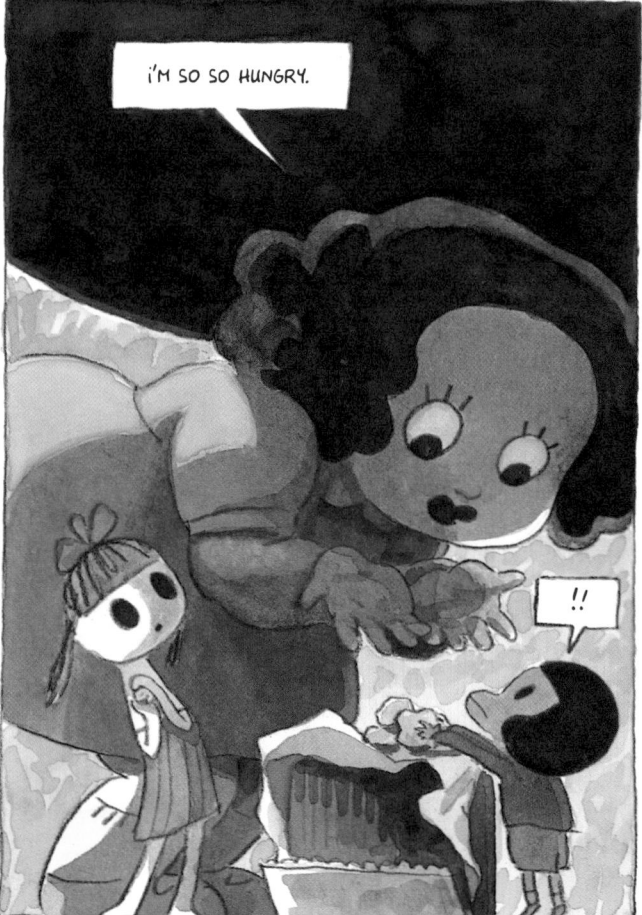

I'M SO SO HUNGRY.

!!

16

HECTOR?

C'MON, LET'S GO EAT.

NAAW!

JEEZ, COME ON!

NAAAH!!

YOU'RE SUCH A PAIN!

HECTOR!

MY DEAR, HERE YOU ARE.

i WONDERED WHAT HAPPENED TO YOU.

WERE YOU WORRIED ABOUT ME?

NO, i...WELL, MAYBE A BiT.

OH, YOU SHOULDN'T HAVE. i CAN TAKE CARE OF MYSELF YOU KNOW.

BUT THIS WHOLE SiTUATION IS SO STRANGE!

UH...THAT'S
ENOUGH FOR TODAY.

WHAT A MESS!

WE'VE GOT NOTHING LEFT TO EAT!

OH! PLIM, I'M SO HAPPY!

PLIM!!

DO I KNOW YOU?

...WE COULD USE SOME ROPE.

HEY, I KNOW!

NAAAH!!

HEE HEE.

WHHAA!

?

WHWHWH WHAAA!!

HEY THERE, WHAT'S WRONG? ARE YOU SAD?

EHEU HEU!

WHERE'S YOUR MOMMA? DID SHE DISAPPEAR?

EHEU!

DON'T WORRY, BABY, I'LL TAKE CARE OF YOU.

GOO!

FRRRTCH...

BZZZZZZZ

HEE HEE! THAT TICKLES!

THIS IS FUN!...

I'M HUNGRY.

WE'RE HUNGRY TOO, YOU KNOW...MAYBE AURORA WILL FIND FOOD FOR US TODAY.

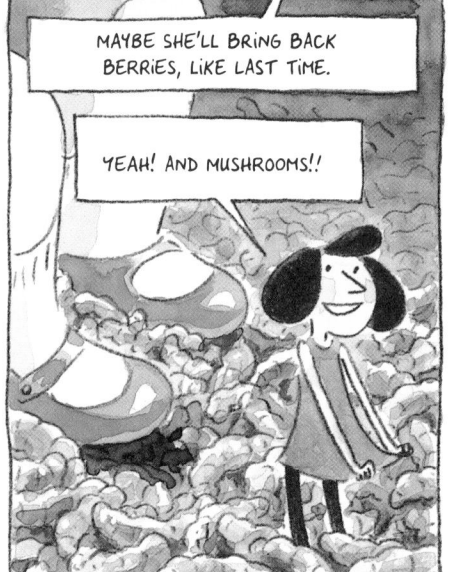

MAYBE SHE'LL BRING BACK BERRIES, LIKE LAST TIME.

YEAH! AND MUSHROOMS!!

NO, WE SAID NO MORE MUSHROOMS, REMEMBER? SOME OF THEM ARE DEAD-LY.

OH, RIGHT, THAT'S TRUE. POOR JOSEPHINE, MARGO, AND AGATHA. I LIKED THEM.

AND POOR SWEETIE, ADELAIDE, AND MIMI...

AND JUJU AND ASTRID, TUBBY, CELESTE, AND STINKER.

...AND WILSON.

YOU KNOW WHAT? WE NEED TO FIND OTHER THINGS TO EAT...

SO HUNGRY.

SURE, BUT WHAT?

i MEAN, WE CAN'T BE LiKE THAT PiG. GROSS!

EATING FLIES AND MAGGOTS!

DISGUSTING!

SO SO HUNGRY.

HEY! WH...??

WHAT DID YOU JUST DO!?

WANNA PLAY? LOOK, iT'S LiKE i'M PREGNANT.

HA HA! ALL RiGHT!

OH!! i CAN FEEL THE BABY MOVE!

CALL ME MOMMY!

ik ik iiik!

OH, UH...NO THANKS, I'LL PASS ON THE MUD. I'M NOT HUNGRY ANYMORE.

BUT I'D BE GLAD TO TAKE A FEW BERRIES HOME!

THANKS SO MUCH FOR HAVING ME!

I NEED TO GO NOW.

!

TAPATA TAPATAP

SKEEEK! EEEEK!

DON'T WORRY, I'LL BE BACK LATER. I PROMISE.

THERE, THAT'S BETTER, HUH?

SHE'S BACK!

ARE YOU OKAY? DID THE MOUSE TRY TO SCRATCH YOU WITH HIS POINTY CLAWS?

NO, NO, EVERYTHING WAS FINE.

DON'T EAT THEM ALL! LEAVE SOME FOR THE OTHERS.

HURRAY!

HE'S STRANGE, BUT HE'S KIND. I BET HE'S GLAD TO HAVE NEW NEIGHBORS!

IN ANY CASE, I THINK HE'LL HELP US FIND MORE STRAWBERRIES...

YOU'RE THE BEST! YOU EVEN UNDERSTAND MOUSE LANGUAGE!

STOP COPYING ME ALL THE TIME!

THIS IS MY IDEA! GO AWAY!!

MPFF...

THAT WAS A REALLY GREAT IDEA!

YEAH...REALLY!

GRMMMBBLE

CHEEP CHEEP

CHEEP
CHEEP
CHEEP

CHEEP

CHEEP

CHEEP

CHEEP

CHEEP CHEEP

RRHHH

i GUESS iT WASN'T SUCH
A GOOD iDEA AFTER ALL.

NO, iT REALLY WASN'T
SUCH A GOOD iDEA.

?

MiND NOT REPEATiNG
EVERYTHiNG i SAY?

ALL CLEAR! NO DANGER IN SIGHT!!

...HHHHH   HH...UHHHHHH   H...   HHHHHHHHHHH...

HH... HHHHHHHHH...

HOW ABOUT A SHAKE?

C'MON, GIMME!

SNAP

NOW THE OTHER ONE, C'MON!

OH! HELLO!

WE KEEP MEETING, BUT WE'VE NEVER INTRODUCED OURSELVES. I'M AURORA!

I...I'M T-TIMOTHY...

YOU KEEP TO YOURSELF A LOT, DON'T YOU? YOU SHOULD COME JOIN US AT THE CAMP.

NO...THE OTHERS SCARE ME...

THERE'S NO NEED TO BE AFRAID!

NO...ACTUALLY, YES...I'M DIFFERENT FROM THE OTHERS. I FEEL LIKE SOMETHING BAD COULD HAPPEN...

DON'T WORRY, TIMOTHY. I PROMISE, NOTHING BAD WILL EVER HAPPEN AGAIN. YOU HAVE MY WORD.

I'M DOING EVERYTHING I CAN TO MAKE THINGS LIKE THEY WERE BEFORE. TRUST ME?

UH...YES.

I'M GOING TO GO NOW. BUT IF YOU GET TOO LONELY, COME JOIN US, ALL RIGHT?

OKAY.

33

C'MON!

LET'S GO!

WHAT DO YOU ALL THINK YOU'RE DOING?

WE'RE TRYING TO TEACH HIM TRICKS!

BUT... HOW COME?

...

HEY! HOW ABOUT WE HUNT FOR PEBBLES?!

YEAAHH! LET'S GO LOOK FOR PEBBLES!!

HELLO.

HELLO.

WHAT'S WRONG WITH YOUR HAND?

I SCRATCHED MYSELF ON A PLANT. IT'S SUPER ITCHY.

OKAY, I'LL KEEP AN EYE ON THE PLANTS, TOO.

WOULD YOU? THANKS.

THE ANTS GO MARCHING ONE BY ONE, ♪HURRAH! HURRAH! ♪ THE ANTS GO MARCHING ONE BY ONE ♪ HURRAH! HURRAH! ♫

HI, AURORA! HOW'S THE BERRY PICKING GOING?

UH, ALL RIGHT... AND THE HUNTING?

GREAT! OF COURSE, YOU'VE GOT TO BE PATIENT...STAGS AND WILD BOARS ARE QUICK AND SMART. YOU CAN'T JUST WALK UP TO THEM.

BUT TRUST ME... CHOMP CHOMP...WE'LL ALL BE EATING A NICE ROAST IN NO TIME!

I DON'T DOUBT IT FOR A SECOND.

AURORA, I'VE BEEN WANTING TO SAY...

YES?

WE HAVEN'T SEEN EACH OTHER AS MUCH AS I'D LIKE THESE LAST FEW DAYS...

BUT YOU'RE ALWAYS ON MY MIND, EVERY MOMENT OF THE DAY! EVEN IN THE HEAT OF THE CHASE, MY THOUGHTS RUSH TO YOU!

!!

HOW'S IT GOING?

FINE. DON'T WORRY, I'VE GOT EVERYTHING UNDER CONTROL.

HERE, HAVE SOME BERRIES.

NO THANKS...KEEP THEM FOR THOSE WHO NEED THEM MOST.

OH, THAT'S SO NICE OF YOU!

PLIM, I WANTED TO TELL YOU...YOU KNOW, I REALLY APPRECIATE EVERYTHING YOU'RE DOING.

WE COULDN'T MANAGE WITHOUT YOU...THANKS, HUH? FROM THE BOTTOM OF MY HEART...

DON'T MENTION IT.

WHEN WE'RE DONE, I'LL GET SOME WOOD TO FORTIFY OUR SHELTER. WE'LL BE NICE AND SAFE.

GOOD IDEA!

SLURP

PLOP PLOP

WELL, HELLO, AURORA! HOW DO YOU LIKE MY DRESS?

IT'S VERY PRETTY.

i KNOW! i'M MAKING iT WiTH FLY WiNGS...iT'S TAKING FOR-EV-ER.

iT LOOKS LIKE A WEDDING GOWN!

DOES iT? i HADN'T NOTiCED!

BUT THEN...iT'S DARK iN HERE. iT'S HARD TO SEW PROPERLY.

iF YOU LIKE, i'LL TRY TO PUT iN SOME WiNDOWS TOMORROW.

CAN'T YOU DO iT SOONER? OH WELL, i GUESS YOU'RE DOING YOUR BEST.

SEE YOU TOMORROW!

SWEET BUT A BiT SLOW ON THE UPTAKE.

HEE HEE HEE!

PPFFF!

39

IT WAS HIGH TIME FOR A BATH. AND MY DRESS IS ALL STAINED.

FLAP FLAP

OH!

HAVE YOU COME TO FRESHEN UP AS WELL?

WAIT!...

FLAPFLAPFLAP

?

TAPATAPATAP

AAH!!

BRAAM!!

SKRAAATCH!
SKRAAATCH!

SKRATCH
SKRATCH
SKRATCH
SKIN·
J···

THE THING I LIKED ABOUT YOU RIGHT AWAY IS, YOU'RE COOL. YOU'RE SUPER COOL!

THAT'S RIGHT.

BECAUSE I... HUH?! PLIM!

YEAH? WHAT'S THE MATTER?

O...ON YOUR...SHOULDER!!

HOLD STILL! IT COULD STING YOU!

!!

I'LL MAKE IT COME THIS WAY! HEY! HEEEY!

YOO-HOO!!

IT'S WORKING!! I'M GONNA GET IT AS FAR AWAY AS POSSIBLE!

DON'T WORRY ABOUT ME, PLIM! I...I CAN MANAGE!

EEEEEE!!

HEY, YOU! COME CARRY MY WOOD!

A BIT OF MOSS ON THE GROUND AND IT'LL BE PERFECT.

HECTOR WILL BE HAPPY. i THINK HE'S GOING TO LIKE IT HERE.

BUT ENOUGH TALK. THERE'S LOTS MORE HOUSES TO BUILD!

EVERYBODY NEEDS A LITTLE HOUSE, iT'S IMPORTANT...

i DON'T LIKE THAT FLY.

HOW COME?

HEY, AURORA... WHY ARE YOU CRYING?

?!...i DON'T KNOW...

AURORA?

...i DON'T FEEL SO GOOD.

EEEEEEEEE!!!

EEEEE

HHHH...HHHH
NIGHTMARE...

HHH...HHHH
NIGHTMARE!

WHEW!

RISE AND SHIIINE!!

HALT!

HEY, NICE HEADDRESS.

HAND IT OVER.

...MMMH I'M THIRSTY...

I...I'LL GO GET SOME DEW WATER.

STILL STUCK?

IT'S BEEN SIX DAYS.

HALT!

I TOLD HER IT WAS TOO SMALL.

I KNOW, BUT SHE REALLY WANTED TO HAVE TEA WITH NADINE AND PIPPA.

FLAP
FLAP
FLAP

FLAP FLAP

WAIT, I'M COMING!

HOW CAN I HELP?

THE SCISSORS!

NOW, CUT!

CUT THE WING, FAST!

CR...
CRATCH!

NOW THIS ONE, HURRY!

SCREEEETCH!

HE WON'T BE ABLE TO GO VERY FAR.

I'LL FINISH TAMING HIM WHEN HE GETS TIRED OF HOPPING AROUND.

YOU'RE LEAVING FOR GOOD THIS TIME, AREN'T YOU?

THE OTHERS ARE LUCKY TO HAVE YOU, YOU KNOW.

HAVE YOU FOUND IT?

HOLD ON!

MPF

HA!

BUT IT'S NOT GLOWING!

WAIT!

AAAAAH!

WHAT'S THAT?

I'M THROWING A PARTY.

A PARTY?

FOR US AND THE FOREST ANIMALS.

HERE, THIS IS YOUR INVITATION.

YOU NEED TO COME, OKAY? WE'VE GOT TO MEET OUR NEIGHBORS IF WE ALL WANT TO GET ALONG.

HNNFFF!

SBLURF!

i GUESS iT WAS ROTTEN.

LOOK, THAT ONE'S BETTER!

HEY! YOU TWO!

C'MERE, SiNCE YOU'RE NOT DOiNG ANYTHiNG. ZELiE NEEDS HELP SEWiNG HER DRESS.

UH, ACTUALLY, WE'RE BUSY... WE'RE CHOOSiNG A GiFT FOR AURORA.

iT'S TO THANK HER FOR iNViTiNG US TO HER FOREST PARTY!

COME ON! THiS'LL TAKE TWO MiNUTES! DON'T BE SO SELFiSH!

FiNE, SETTLED. FOLLOW ME.

WHAT?...OKAY, BUT...

UHH...CAN YOU BRiNG THE APPLE TO AURORA, PLEASE?

A SEED WOULD DO TOO. i THiNK i'D LiKE iT iF SOMEONE GAVE ME A SEED.

HEY, YOU! WHAT'RE YOU DOING HERE?

i SEE...AURORA GAVE YOU AN INVITATION TOO.

BUT YOU'RE NOT GOING TO THE PARTY LIKE THAT, ARE YOU? YOU LOOK LIKE A BEGGAR. HERE, i'LL DO YOUR HAIR.

UH, NO, i...

C'MON...YOU DON'T WANT TO HURT AURORA'S FEELINGS, DO YOU?

i...i'M A MONSTER.

WELL, THAT'S TRUE!

i DON'T DESERVE TO LIVE HERE, WITH ALL OF YOU.

HEY, i'VE GOT AN iDEA! YOU TWO, GET THE PENCiL CASE. WE'LL HAVE A BURiAL! THiS WiLL BE GREAT.

...OKAY, LiE DOWN iNSiDE, AND YOU'LL BE DEAD.

...ALL RiGHT...

NOW COVER HER WiTH EARTH.

i'LL PRETEND TO PRAY.

MNMMMNMMMNNNNMMNNNMMNN

THAT'S ONE CEREMONY DONE. VERY, VERY GOOD.

WHAT DO WE DO NOW?

iT'S LATE...LET'S GO HOME.

GOO?

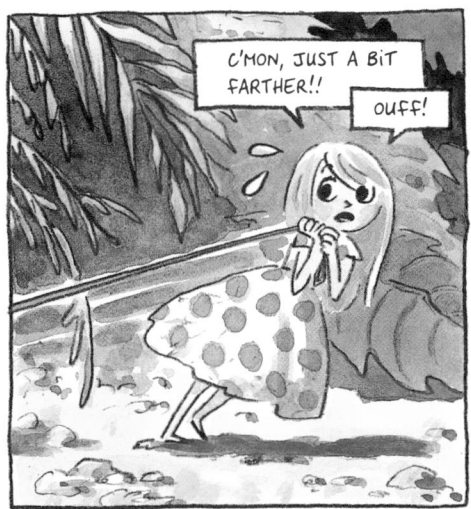

C'MON, JUST A BIT FARTHER!!

OUFF!

MPFF!

FRRRRRR

THERE...

I'M HERE! I'VE BROUGHT A LATECOMER.

...THE OTHERS HAVEN'T ARRIVED?

PLIM, HECTOR, TIMOTHY... THEY PROMISED THEY'D BE HERE!

AURORA, DON'T YOU THINK WE SHOULD JUST EAT AND GO?...

NO, NO, WE'LL WAIT A BIT LONGER...

I'M SURE THEY'LL BE HERE ANY MOMENT.

EXCEPT IT'LL BE DARK. THAT'S TOO BAD.

WAIT!!

NOT YET! BACK OFF!

i SAID, WAIT!

NO...

Hi, ZELiE.

HEY, AURORA...

SO, HOW'S THE PARTY COMING ALONG?

...?

ARE YOU SURE?...

iT...iT WAS YESTERDAY!

YOUR INVITATION WASN'T CLEAR ABOUT THE DATE.

HERE, HAVE A SEAT AND TELL ME HOW IT WENT.

iT WAS TERRIBLE! THE ANIMALS BEHAVED LIKE... LIKE BEASTS!

ONE OF THEM EVEN PEED ON THE TABLE!

AND NOBODY CAME, NOT EVEN TIMOTHY! EVEN THOUGH i SPECIFICALLY TOLD HER THE TIME.

HOW THOUGHTLESS! YOU MUST HAVE FELT HUMILIATED.

HECTOR DiDN'T COME EITHER!

OH!

GET ME SOME THREAD, WOULD YOU?

AURORA, YOU KNOW HOW BOYS CAN BE...I'M SURE HECTOR DIDN'T MEAN TO UPSET YOU.

YOU THINK?

I'M CERTAIN. HE PROBABLY MISUNDERSTOOD, THAT'S ALL.

YOU KNOW WHAT? I'LL GO TALK TO HIM! MAYBE THAT'LL REASSURE YOU.

OH!

THANKS, ZELIE, TH... THAT'S VERY KIND OF YOU.

DON'T THANK ME YET! YOU NEVER KNOW WITH MEN...

?

IT'S STARTING, HURRY!!

WHAT DO YOU MEAN? WHAT'S STARTING?

HUUURRY!

HEE HEE HEE!!

COME ON, WHAT IS IT?

THERE, SEE FOR YOURSELF!

OH, LOOK WHO'S HERE!

GOOD, CUZ WE'VE GOT SOMETHING FOR YOU.

GO AWAY. i DON'T WANT TO SEE ANYBODY.

HEY, GUYS, OVER HERE!!

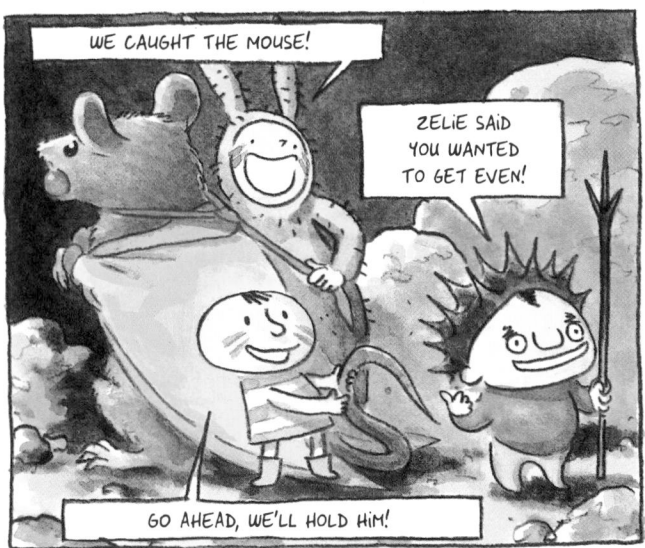

WE CAUGHT THE MOUSE!

ZELiE SAID YOU WANTED TO GET EVEN!

GO AHEAD, WE'LL HOLD HiM!

WHAT'RE YOU WAITiNG FOR?!

DO YOU WANT HiM TO PEE ON YOU AGAiN OR WHAT?

HEE HEE HEE!

HA HA!

DO iT!!

GO TELL THE OTHERS WE FOUND FOOD.

OKAY...BURP...LET'S FIND ZELIE.
i KEPT THE HEART FOR HER.

BUT IT'S VERY FAR, AND I DON'T SEE HOW I CAN—

YOU'RE MY PRINCE, SO YOU **HAVE** TO SERVE ME, DON'T YOU?

UH...

YES, OF COURSE! I... I'M YOUR PRINCE!

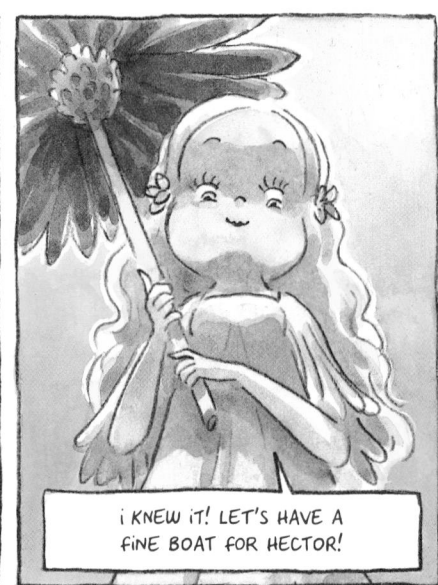

I KNEW IT! LET'S HAVE A FINE BOAT FOR HECTOR!

UGH, ARE YOU EVEN TRYING?!

WHAT'S TAKING SO LONG?!

IT'S THAT...I BETTER NOT FALL IN, I CAN'T...

?!!

THERE'S SOMETHING IN THE WATER!!

HECTOR, ENOUGH. JUST GET THE RIBBON!

SPLASH SPLASH SPLASH SPLASH

AAAHH!!

PLUNK

HERE, I'VE GOT IT!

I EMPTIED IT. EXCEPT FOR SOME SMALL SCRATCHES INSIDE, IT'S LIKE NEW.

VERY GOOD. IT WOULD HAVE BEEN UNFAIR TO GIVE HECTOR LESS OF A CEREMONY THAN TIMOTHY.

NOW, LET US GRIEVE THE SAD FATE OF MY DECEASED HUSBAND.

HECTOR?!

BOO HOO HOO HOO HECTOR!

POOR ZELIE!

WHAT'RE YOU DOING HERE?

i DON'T WANT TO LIVE WITH THE OTHERS ANYMORE.

COME.

YOU CAN SPEND THE NIGHT HERE, BUT NOT A SOUND.

HE'S RIGHT NEXT DOOR.

LOOK FOR YOURSELF.

!

HELLO, JANE!

DO YOU LIKE IT?

...YOU GOT THIS IN HIS HOUSE, DIDN'T YOU?

YOU DON'T HAVE TO WORRY. i WAS CAREFUL.

i'M TELLING YOU, HE'S DANGEROUS.

...AND HE STINKS WORSE THAN ANYTHING!!

HE DOES?

THE SOONER i FIND ANOTHER PLACE, THE BETTER.

...iT'LL BE DiFFiCULT, AS LONG AS iT'S SO COLD OUT.

AT LEAST iT'S WARM HERE, AND THERE'S FOOD.

PLIC

SCRATCH
SCRATCH

JANE! i SAW SOMETHING!
COME QUICK!!

WHAT ARE YOU
TALKING ABOUT?

JUST COME,
PLEASE!!

IS IT ZELIE?

...THEY'RE HEADED THIS WAY.

AND THOSE IDIOTS ARE SINGING... THEY'LL GIVE US AWAY!

JANE?!

STAY HERE... I'LL TRY TO DO SOMETHING!

JANE, WAIT FOR ME!

AURORA, WHAT A SURPRISE!

WE THOUGHT YOU WERE DEAD.

...WHERE IS JANE? THAT'S HER ROBIN.

JANE? DON'T KNOW HER.

HELLO, AURORA!...

WHAT A DUMP. WE'LL NEED TO FIX IT UP, QUICK.

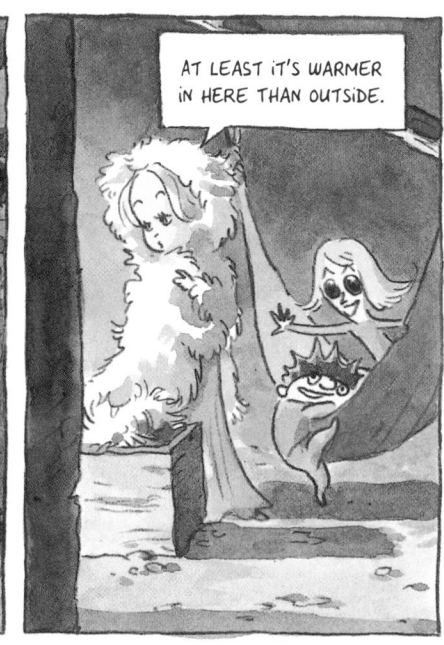

AT LEAST IT'S WARMER IN HERE THAN OUTSIDE.

YOU CAN'T STAY HERE! ...THIS IS MY PLACE...

NO! NOT THERE!

IT'S DANGEROUS. THAT'S WHERE HE LIVES! THE...THE GIANT. HE'S VERY MEAN!...

IT'S MUCH WARMER HERE!

ZELIE!

YOU NEED TO CALL HER PRINCESS NOW.

IT'S BEST TO KEEP QUIET OR THEY'LL MAKE YOU MISERABLE. BUT I'LL BE YOUR FRIEND.

YOU'RE BACK, FINALLY.

WE FIGURED HUNGER WOULD GET THE BEST OF YOU.

YOU'RE TOO LATE, THERE'S NOTHING LEFT. THAT'LL TEACH YOU.

YOU KNOW, AURORA, YOU NEED TO DO WHAT YOU'RE TOLD IF YOU WANT TO STAY HERE WITH US.

YOU CAN START BY WASHING OUR BOOTS...AND THEY BETTER BE DRY BY TOMORROW.

DID YOU HEAR HER?

SHUSH, PLIM. I'LL HELP HER. SHE'S NOT USED TO THIS YET.

YOU'LL SEE, IT'S EASY ENOUGH ONCE YOU ADJUST!

THANKS...

WAIT, I'LL BE BACK...

PLIM, I NEED TO TALK TO YOU!

I'M BORED ALREADY.

I KNOW A SECRET PLACE...I'D LIKE TO SHARE IT WITH YOU, LIKE BEFORE, BUT IN EXCHANGE YOU NEED TO HELP ME KEEP IT SECRET FROM ZELIE, OKAY?

MAYBE.

I'LL BE YOUR SERVANT TOO, IF YOU LIKE.

OKAY THEN. WHERE IS IT?

IT'LL BE OUR VERY OWN SECRET, ALL RIGHT? PROMISE?

CROSS MY HEART AND HOPE TO DIE.

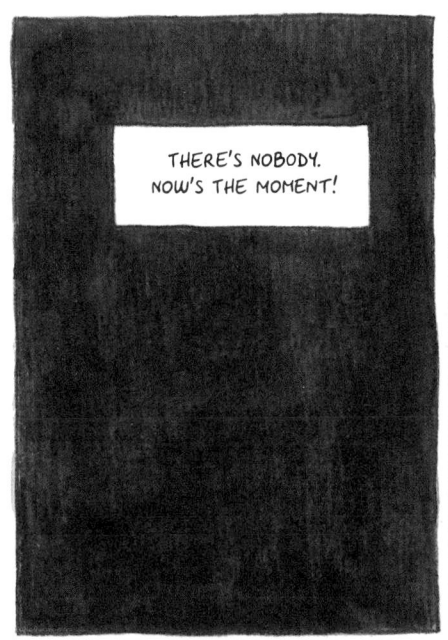

THERE'S NOBODY.
NOW'S THE MOMENT!

OVER HERE,
ZELIE!

HEY, THIS IS NICE!

AND IT'S SO MUCH WARMER THAN THAT DINGY SHED.

AURORA WAS
HIDING IT!

THAT WASN'T
VERY SMART.

BUT YOU'VE NEVER BEEN
TOO BRIGHT, HAVE YOU?...
THAT'S YOUR PROBLEM, AURORA.

I'LL THINK OF A PUNISHMENT...TO SET AN EXAMPLE.

SPECS, COME GIVE ME A MASSAGE!

YES, PRINCESS. COMING.

AURORA?

KLONG!

CLACK!

HEY, WHAT'S ALL THIS?

I'LL NEED TO REBUILD
MY LITTLE NEST...

IT'S ALL RIGHT. I'VE GOT
PLENTY OF TIME.

THAT MEAL YOU'RE MAKING
FOR US SMELLS GOOD.

MY SWEET PRINCE.